Baby Animals on the Farm

By Liza Alexander
Illustrated by Tom Cooke

Featuring Jim Henson's Sesame Street Muppets

A SESAME STREET/GOLDEN PRESS BOOK
Published by Western Publishing Company, Inc.
in conjunction with Children's Television Workshop

"Hello, everybodee! It is I, Grover. Would you like to meet some cute and fuzzy baby animals? Of course you would! Lots have just been born on the farm because it is spring! The baby animals will have the warm summer to grow big and strong before winter comes. Come along, now!"

"Greetings, Grover!" said the Count. "Meet six wonderful kittens!"

"Hello, Count," said Grover. "Hello, little kitties. You are very cute and furry, but you are not blue!"

"Let's count all the kitties!" said the Count. "One tiger-striped mommy cat. One calico kitten. Two striped kittens. Two black kittens with mittens. There should be three black kittens with mittens. Oh, no! One of the adorable kittens with mittens is missing!"

"Oh, my goodness!" said Grover. "Count, do not worry! I, Grover, will search high and low for the missing black kitty with mitties."

"Mew!" said the kittens.

"Meow!" said the cat.

"Bow-wow!" barked Barkley.

"Here are Ernie and Bert at the duckie pond," said Grover. "Hello, Ernie! Hello, Bert! Have you perhaps seen a black kitty with mitties? He is missing from the barn."

"Why, no, I'm afraid we haven't seen any kitty," said Bert.

"Hi there, Grover," said Ernie.

"Quack!" said the duck.

"Quack, quack!" said the ducklings.

"Squeak, squeak!" squeaked Rubber Duckie.

"How did you know I was at the chicken coop?" asked Big Bird.

"Just lucky, I guess," answered Grover. "Have you seen a cute little black kitty with mitties?"

"No, Grover. Nobody here but us chickens! Here, chicky-chick-chicks!" called Big Bird.

"Aha!" said Grover. "The chicks just hatched from those eggs. There is the mommy hen and there is the daddy rooster. They must be so proud!"

"Cock-a-doodle-doo!" crowed the rooster.

"Bawk!" clucked the hen.

"Cheep, cheep!" sang the chicks.

"Now, where is that kitty? Maybe the sweet little bunnies will know," said Grover. "Oh, you are so cute when you wiggle your noses. I will feed the bunnies some tasty carrots.

"This is my favorite bunny. Her name is Babbie Rabbit."

"Crunch, crunch!" said Babbie.

"Yoo-hoo, Herry Monster!" Grover called. "Is there a little black kitty with mitties anywhere in this field?"

"No, there are no kittens here," said Herry Monster. "Say hello to Maysie the cow and her calf Seymour."

"How do you do!" said Grover.

"Moo!" said Maysie.

"And now for the barnyard," said Grover. "Look, there is the daddy gander. And there are the baby goslings. Look at them walking one by one behind the mommy goose."

"Honk!" said the goose and the gander.

"Honk, honk!" said the goslings.

"Honk, honk, honk!" honked the Honkers.

"Let us visit the pig pen now. Maybe the little kitty
is here," said Grover. "Here, kitty, kitty!"

"Furface," said Oscar, "kittens don't like mud. Pigs like
mud because it's cool. And Grouches love mud because it's
yucchy!"

"What adorable piggies," said Grover. "Did you know that a mommy pig is called a sow? Look at all the little piglets running lickety-split to their mommy," he said. "She's telling her babies that it is time for lunch."

"Oink!" grunted the sow.

"Oink, oink!" squealed the piglets.

"Meet the sheep family," said Grover. "These are lambs. They are the baby sheep."

"A daddy sheep is called a ram, and a mommy sheep is called a ewe," said Prairie Dawn.

"The lambs are so soft and woolly," said Grover. "Ooooh! Soft as a kitty. That reminds me, where is that kitty with mitties?"

"Baa!" said the ram and the ewe.

"Baa, baa!" said the lambs.

"I hope the little black kitty with mitties is here at the paddock," said Grover. "Horses and donkeys play in the paddock. Baby horses and baby donkeys are called foals."

"No fooling," said Cookie Monster.

"Look at the foal running and kicking with his long and spindly legs," said Grover.

"Neigh!" said the horse.
"Neigh, neigh!" said the foal.
"Hee, haw!" said the donkeys.
"Caw, caw!" crowed the crow.
"Cowabunga!" said Cookie Monster.

"What a steep hill this is," said Grover. "I wish I could find the kitty with mitties up here! But it is worth the climb to meet the mommy goat and her babies, who are called kids.

"Pant, pant!" said Grover.

"Maaaaaaa!" said the goat.

"Maaaaaaa! Maaaaaaa!" said the kids.

"Have you seen an adorable black kitty with mitties up here in this tree?" asked Grover.

"No, Grover," said Betty Lou. "Only these baby robins. Look, but don't touch. The babies just hatched out of eggs."

"How sweet!" said Grover.

"Tweet!" sang the mommy bird.

"Tweet, tweet!" sang the baby birds.

"Oh, I am so tired!" said Grover. "I have just enough energy left to introduce you to the mommy dog and all her puppies. Oh, joy, there is the missing black kitty with mitties. You little scoundrel! You have probably been playing here with the puppy dogs all along."

"Woof!" barked the dog.

"Yip, yip!" yapped the puppies.

"Mew, mew!" meowed the kitten.

"Oh, I am so sad that we have to leave now!" said Grover. "Here we go, back to Sesame Street! We will come back to the farm next spring to meet more new baby animals.

"Good-bye, everybodee!"

"Oink, oink!"

"Cock-a-doodle-doo!"

"Hee, haw!"

"Bawk!"

"Cheep, cheep!"

"Neigh!"

"Crunch!"

"Honk, honk!"

"Woof, woof!"

"Meow!"

"Yip, yip!"

"Mew!"

"Tweet, tweet!"

"Caw, caw!"

"Maaaaa!"

"Baa, baa!"

"Moo!"

"Quack, quack!"

ABCDEFGHIJ